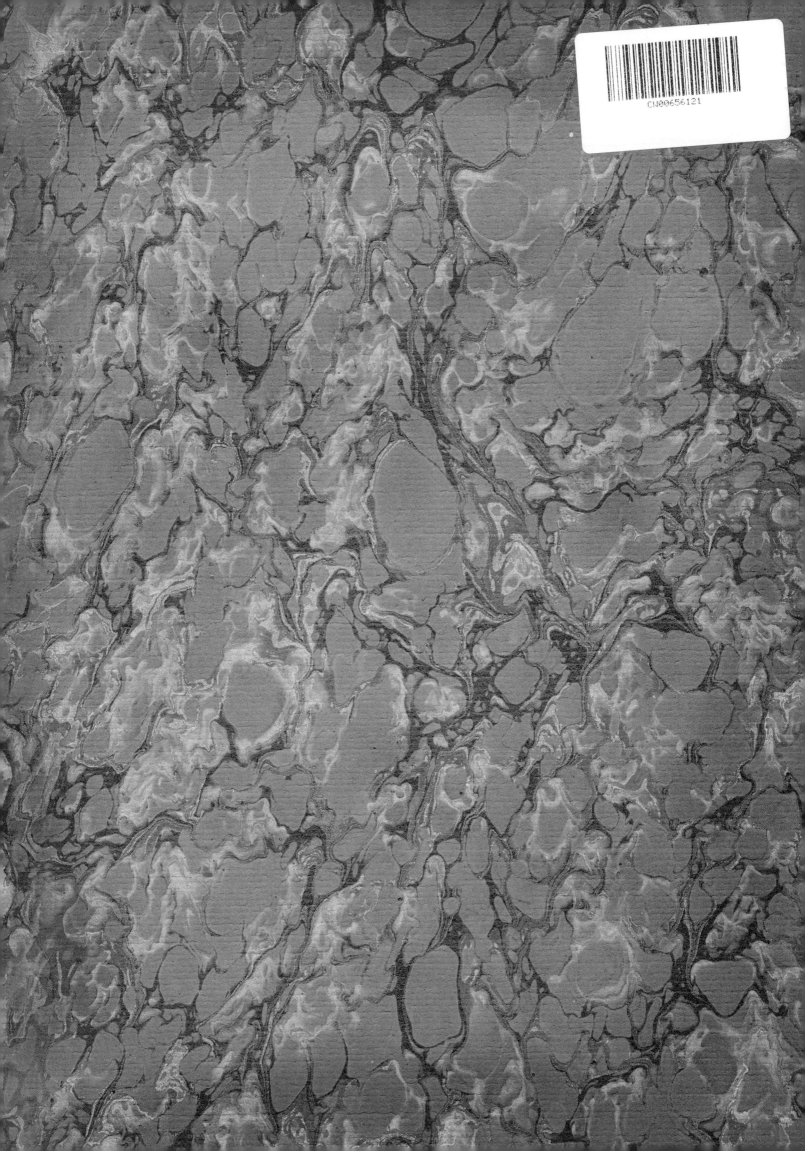
CN00656121

The Pressed Fairy Journal
of Madeline Cottington

by Brian and Wendy Froud

ABRAMS

NEW YORK

Brian and Wendy would like to thank:

Lillian Todd-Jones, Virginia Lee, and Howard Gayton, for their invaluable contribution to the making of this book;
Hazel Brown, for the exquisite calligraphy;
Scarlet Sinclair, for the beautiful bee tattoo—www.scarlettattoos.com;
Terry Jones, for being at the birth of Quentin and Angelica;
Terri Windling, for unwavering encouragement;
as always, thank you Howard Reeves, for being our wonderful editor;
and to all of the people at Abrams Books who believe in us and help us achieve what we do—we thank you!

This book is dedicated to the bees and the fairies.

Editor: Howard Reeves
Book Design: Brian Froud
Design Manager: Danny Maloney
Production Manager: Anet Sirna-Bruder

Library of Congress Control Number: 2015956323

ISBN: 978-1-4197-2085-7

Text copyright © 2016 Wendy Froud
Illustrations and photographs copyright © 2016 Brian Froud

Published in 2016 by Abrams, an imprint of ABRAMS. All rights reserved. No portion of this book may be reproduced, stored in a retrieval system, or transmitted in any form or by any means, mechanical, electronic, photocopying, recording, or otherwise, without written permission from the publisher.

Printed and bound in China
10 9 8 7 6 5 4 3 2 1

Abrams books are available at special discounts when purchased in quantity for premiums and promotions as well as fundraising or educational use. Special editions can be created to specification. For details, contact specialsales@abramsbooks.com or the address below.

ABRAMS
The Art of Books

115 West 18th Street
New York, NY 10011
www.abramsbooks.com

The RSPCF (The Royal Society For The Prevention of Cruelty to Fairies) have certified that no fairies were injured, maimed, or killed in the making of this book. All images of the fairies are only psychic impressions that remain imprinted on the pages after the fairies fly away, free from harm.

Lady Angelica Cottington was the first person to discover the mischievous marvel of fairies that often competed with each other to produce more and more artistic shapes and outrageous poses.

Foreword

It was my dubious honor to introduce to an unsuspecting (and soon-to-be horrified) world, the extraordinary Lady Cottington and her now infamous book of pressed fairies.

At the very first moment of the year 1990, at the stroke of midnight, a rather grubby envelope was pushed under the door of my gypsy caravan, "The Flying Fandango." I had been sitting alone, with the last of the Malmsey wine, and had been trying unsuccessfully to open a celebratory tin of sardines. I was then completely unaware of the life-changing properties of the envelope's contents. There was no note or explanation within the envelope, only a scrap of paper.

After many months of careful study of the pressed flowers stuck onto the scrap of paper, one Thursday I noticed that what I assumed was a vegetable or fruit stain was seemingly a miniscule form of a fairy. Imagine my excitement at the discovery. I was inspired to now renew my efforts to open the aforementioned sardine tin, but alas, with no success. I had dedicated my professional career to the pursuit of the actual proof of the existence of fairies. Was it possible I had now found it? I lay for days in the dark space of my caravan, feverish, often singing loudly in a falsetto voice the old songs of Marie Lloyd.

The following Tuesday at 9:37 A.M., simultaneously the fever broke, I sneezed, and another envelope was delivered. It was from the "Cottington Archive." I had never heard of it before but I was soon to learn that they were a shadowy and secretive organization. Suffice to say they swore me to complete secrecy of who they are and where they are, and I *have* completely forgotten the sherry trifle and Miss Darymble's revelations that evening at 6 Mafeking Villas, Dreary Lane, Bovey Tracy.

Gradually the Archive released to me more and more astonishing documents pertaining to the Cottington family. These have been published over the years. The first, *Lady Cottington's Pressed Fairy Book*, reveals in its disclosures the life of the Victorian Lady Angelica's lifelong pursuit of fairies and the comprehensive collection of psychic pressings she made.

As more and more material from the Archive accumulated—sometimes left in old paper bags on the roof of the caravan, or in rusting biscuit tins under the wheel—the existence of Angelica's twin brother Quentin emerged, along with his early scientific work investigating psychic olfactory-phenomena. His work was published in *Strange Stains and Mysterious Smells*, now avidly sought after by collectors in the hope that all copies can be destroyed.

The Archive was now sending me more evidence of another family member, Euphemia, who had triumphed in capturing photographic evidence of fairies before she mysteriously disappeared. Much of this material was left within the crust of meat pies. It was an arduous, if tasty, work to lick the gravy (I mean restore the photographs) so they could be viewed in the published work, *Lady Cottington's Fairy Album*.

By 2005 the Archive taunted me with a bundle of letters wrapped in string, unpaid bills, and demands from local wine merchants. The Archive begged that I should destroy them after reading, but unfortunately I forgot and published them in *Lady Cottington's Pressed Fairy Letters*. The estates of J. M. Barrie, Rasputin, Sir Arthur Conan Doyle, and William Shakespeare have all attempted to withdraw their contributions, without success...yet.

It has often been my onerous task as the recipient of so much Cottingtonalia, to examine, scrutinize, and verify the often distasteful squashings and odiferous smears, but I continue to do it with a noble sense of scientific inquiry, for I have long ago abandoned all hope of financial reward or knighthood (or an open sardine tin). All I can realistically hope for is a third-rate rest home near the gasworks in the less salubrious sector of Budleigh Salterton.

The series of Cottington books may have provoked outrage or indifference from the discerning reader, however, some scholars of the esoteric—notably a group in Oxford known as the "Stinklings"—gather weekly at the Dingly Arms, a rather down-at-heel public house. Here, over hot, buttered crumpets and pints of Bishop's Finger, they conduct fierce, philosophical debates about the various fairy phenomena appearing in my books. Past incumbents of chairman for the Stinklings, known as the Grand Pong, have been Mr. Terry Jones and Professor Ari Berk. Professor Berk used to be an eminent Goblinologist, but now has retired and is an enthusiastic cheese sculptor and no longer attends meetings, Stinkling or otherwise.

I have gratefully become—on a very temporary basis and wearing a little hat of my own devising—a lesser Grand Pong known as a "Little Whiff," and now preside over meetings in a back room of the pub next door, on my own, on the first Thursday of April, every alternative leap year.

This has left me the luxurious time to oversee this new volume in the Cottington saga: *The Pressed Fairy Journal of Madeline Cottington*. This surely must be the most astonishing in its contents. A new and very recent member of the Cottington family helps the reader piece together the poignant relationship between two of the Cottington siblings. The fairies, although still vigorously pursued, are as mischievous as ever.

So, perhaps, here at last is the indisputable evidence of the existence of fairies and their nature. A new generation of Cottington, Madeline is transformed by what she discovers into...Maddi C., Fearless Fairy Hunter!

I have decided, for historical authenticity, to submit this writing as it was sent to me by Brian, who was on a much-needed retreat near Southend-on-Sea. Make of it what you will.

—Wendy Froud
December 10, 2015

Note from the Cottington Archive:
Regrettably, the above writing cannot be fully verified. Brian claims to have written this foreword from a very nice hotel, recommended—and, indeed, paid for—by the Cottington Archive, where there are no distractions from windows, and the walls "are all lovely and soft."

I found some fun stuff to stick in my journal

May 21, 10:30 a.m.

I've never kept a journal before — or a diary or scrapbook or whatever. I don't think I can say "Dear Diary" — it sounds too weird. I could pretend I'm writing to Adeline, the imaginary "evil twin" I had when I was six. Every time I did something REALLY bad, I told Mom and Dad that "Addy" did it. You've got to have SOMEONE to blame (or just talk to) when you're an only child! Or maybe not — maybe I'll just write to myself: Miss Madeline Cottington.

Dad gave me this journal before we left New York. He said a journal was one of the few things he brought with him from England when he left to come to America. He said I should "record my experiences in it." Please. Like I want to record anything on this trip. I keep calling it a trip, but since we're going to be living in London, I guess it's more than a trip. Apparently Dad's job needs him to be there, and Mom of course will go anywhere he goes. And then there's me. I'll be eighteen in November, and I don't know what to do with my life. We didn't find a college for me for September — it was too late to register when Dad decided to move us to England (thanks, Dad) — so maybe I'll get a job or something. Until I can figure out what I'm going to do, I guess I'll just keep this journal and practice my handwriting. Ha! Too bad my laptop gave up — OK, I admit it WAS my fault it fell out of my bedroom window, but it wasn't like I did it on purpose. Dad says I can have a new one for my birthday, but as I said, that's in November. I've got my phone, so I'm still part of the real world, but who am I going to text from here anyway? So, I'm doomed to write — but it's kind of fun writing to myself. And maybe my eyes will start to feel better staring at a book instead of a screen for a while. I'm NOT telling Mom and Dad how bad the floaty things I see are becoming, and NO WAY am I going to wear glasses!

June 2, 9:30 a.m.

Now that we're here in London, the things I keep seeing are getting worse, NOT better like I hoped. I mean, they don't LOOK worse, but there seem to be more of them flying around me all the time. I'm kind of used to seeing them every once in a while, because they've been around as long as I can remember, but since we landed at Heathrow I've seen them most of the time — I mean EVERYWHERE I go — and it's DRIVING ME CRAZY!!! They're always just out of my eye line, on the edges of everything. I told Mom and she said that whatever I do, I can't tell Dad about it being worse. He's SO weird about me seeing things, and Mom says I can't upset him, not when he's starting this job here, whatever THAT is. He can't talk about it. But then, he never talks about his work anyway. I have NO idea what he does. Isn't that crazy? I've never been able to say to anyone that my Dad's a policeman or a scientist or a garbage collector (well, I know he's not a garbage collector or a policeman) or in the secret service. Maybe he IS in the secret service. LOL. Who knows? Not me.

The Cottingtons (that's us) came from here. Not London, but England. My Dad came to America with his sister, Flora, when they were kids, and he's never been back over here as far as I know — it's another thing he doesn't talk about — but he still sounds English. My family goes way, way back in English history. I remember Dad saying that his ancestor, Sir Somebody or Other (I can't remember his name), fought in the Crusades, which is pretty amazing when you think about it, and built a manor house somewhere in Somerset (wherever that is). Does that make us Gentry? Maybe I'm a Lady. Ha! Wikipedia says hardly anything about us or our ancestors. It's like we were swept under the carpet and forgotten.

Where did these blobs come from?
They weren't here before.

While I'm figuring out what to do, maybe I'll dig around in the family history—after all, it's mine too—and see what happened to the rest of the Cottingtons. I mean, we have to have family SOMEWHERE. I don't know what happened to my grandparents, but they must have been around to bring my dad and Aunt Flora over to America if they were only kids. I had one set of them—Mom's parents, Grandy, and Grandpa—but they've gone now. Dad never talks about his parents, and it's not as though I haven't asked him enough times! I don't even know their names. It's like he and Aunt Flora came from another planet (but maybe ENGLAND IS another planet—I don't know yet!). He gets really upset whenever I ask questions about the family. I mean REALLY upset!!! And he looks at me like I'm crazy, especially when I talk about my eye problems—so I don't talk to him about ANYTHING.

Got to stop writing now. My head is killing me, and I can see them all around the corners of my eyes—like they're IN my eyes, even if I know they're not. If they'd just stay still for a second, I'd be able to see better what they are. I could never see them this clearly before I came here, but I can now. It's kind of creepy because they almost look like they have shapes and they were only just blobs or squiggles before. Jeez, it's bad enough having to figure this country out without having to deal with my eye problems getting worse. I like where we're living here, though. It's in a part of London called Belsize Park and there's lots of cool stuff in the big flea market down the road in Camden.

5:00 p.m.

The flea market is always fantastic! I already found the greatest clothes—stuff like my Mom wore when she was my age (she looked pretty cool then): a leather jacket and a pair of amazing lace-up Victorian boots. So many stalls of great stuff! But today was the BEST. I found this one stall that was piled with books. Books everywhere—about plants, people, history, places. New books, old books, and really, really old ones. I asked the vendor if he had books about genealogy, and he did. LOADS! This is England after all. And there in one of the piles I found two books about the Cottingtons! They've got to be about us. How many Cottingtons can there be? I bought them.

SHSPLATT!

He tore up my photo of the bookstall too!

10:00 p.m.

OK. That was too weird—REALLY too weird. I showed Dad one of the books after dinner, and he LOST it. Not the book—his temper! He grabbed it out of my hands and started ripping the pages up, and then he stormed out with it. Mom looked at me like I'd just committed some HUGE crime and said, "Didn't I tell you NEVER to talk about the Cottingtons?" She gets SO upset when Dad loses it like this. When she finished screaming at me, Mom burst into tears, and I was crying and she was crying and Dad was locked in his office room.

I want to go home.

11:00 p.m.

OMG! I just read the other book, "Lady Cottington's Pressed Fairy Album," and if it IS our family, I can see why Dad doesn't want me to know. This is a seriously crazy family, and I think it IS our family back in Victorian times. The books are about seeing fairies!!! This Angelica and the other girl, Effie (her sister or maybe her mother — it isn't clear in the book), both see them flying around their faces, and Effie even talks with them. Like me. Like the things I see!

June 3, 9:30 a.m.

Dad sort of apologized this morning, but didn't explain why he went ballistic on me. He just said the book was rubbish, absolute rubbish, and I shouldn't waste my time reading stuff like that. He said he had thrown the book away. MY book in the trash! He was talking in a really quiet voice, and I could tell he was trying to be calm. I'm glad I didn't show him BOTH books! Later, I looked, but there was no book in his office anywhere.

I'm in my room because I said I had a headache. I DO have a headache, and the eye thing is worse than ever. The blobs are beginning to look like bugs flying around — bees, I guess. I swatted one away, and I could sort of feel it when I hit it with my hand. If they're really there, why can't anyone else see them around me? I feel like a cow that has flies around it — a great big stupid cow with flies around it's eyes. That's me. LOL.

9:00 p.m.

OK, this is getting seriously weird now. I'm not into "Selfies"—I mean, "Look at me—YAY!!!" But when the black blobs started flying around my eyes again this afternoon, they were bigger and kind of more defined than ever. They REALLY looked like they had wings, so I took a selfie to see what would happen, and that's just it: Nothing was there—at first. Then I looked AGAIN, more closely, and they were faint but I could see them! All around my head. And they sure DID have wings and bodies and.....OK, I'm crazy, but they look like fairies!!! They look JUST like fairies!

10:30 p.m.

My Dad lost it again, only in that really calm, creepy way that means he's trying to control himself, where his eyes get big and starry and his mouth goes all small with this tight little smile on it. Mom just didn't say anything when I showed them the photo. I printed it out on my little portable printer so I can keep it in this journal. Anyway, I ran into the living room and showed Mom and Dad—I didn't even think about what they'd say—and Dad took one look and went really pale and walked away, and Mom started crying again. WTF?

OMG! I snapped the book shut on some of those flying things, and I totally can't believe this, but they ARE fairies!!! Really real, but kind of funny looking now that I squashed them. They look just like Angelica's pressed fairies. Amazing! Nobody is going to believe this at all. But it's true! And it's ME pressing them!

This is proof that I'm not imagining it. Isn't it? I'm like Angelica and Effie, and I'm a Cottington. I'm one of THOSE Cottingtons!

Am I crazy?

June 4, 10:00 a.m.
This can't be happening. Dad said they're going to send me back to America to stay with Mom's sister, Aunt Tilly, in Tonawanda, Nebraska. Mom says it's for my own good and I'll thank them someday. What!!!!??? I can't believe this. I mean, WTF? They're sending me by myself. I've only met Aunt Tilly a couple of times, and she's horrible! I can't go to Nebraska. I CAN'T go back to America! I just can't. This ISN'T happening. I'm not doing it. F. this. I'm not.

11:45 p.m.
OK, his office wasn't locked. Why didn't he lock it? The Cottington book was hidden on a shelf and mostly scrumpled and torn up, but I took it away anyway. And I found this stuck to one of the pages.

Cottington Hall
near Mount
Somerset

I'm going to Cottington Hall. I'm not going to go to the middle of nowhere to be with Aunt Tilly. I'm NOT. If I do that I'll go crazy, and if I'm crazy already for seeing fairies, then it does'nt matter, does it? Here's another selfie (I'm going to take my little printer so I can keep printed records of these things). See? They're there again. All around me, and now I can sort of see them for real too. If I hold the journal open just at the right angle, I can press them in it! Well, Angelica said "press," but it's really more like squashing them, except they fly away when I open the book and don't seem to be hurt at all. I think I heard one of them laughing—this little crinkly sound kind of like opening a candy wrapper. Weird.

June 5, 9:00 a.m., on the train.

    I can't believe I did it. I ran away. Well, I didn't run— I snuck out really quietly around 2:00 a.m. this morning, weighed down with stuff: my new clothes and my little printer and journal and the Cottington books and some other things I might need. I walked to Camden looking for a taxi, and it's totally creepy at that time of night—and I lived in New York. I tried not to look at anyone on the street, but some of them REALLY looked at me. Scary!

    The little fairies—I'm going to keep calling them that—left me alone.

    London is HUGE and the streets are all twisty, but I finally got a taxi to the train station. Paddington (like the bear—yay!) is the one for the southwest. The cab driver seemed nice, but he didn't want to take me at first. He asked me if I was sure I wouldn't rather go home, but when I told him I HAD to get to where I was going—that it was really important—he winked at me and said, "All right, love, just making sure. We wouldn't want you ending up somewhere you didn't want to be." Why did he say "we"? Huh. Maybe it's an English thing. When I gave him the money, he handed me a white feather. "For luck," he said. Nice.

    It's kind of strange, but it feels like something is sort of smoothing my path to get to Cottington Hall. I mean, my dad's office is ALWAYS locked, there was money out on his desk (it's not stealing if it's from your dad, is it?), and Mom and Dad both asleep—snoring away. I actually have an address, AND people in the middle of the night were strangely helpful (or maybe English people are just like that). I slept on a bench at Paddington Station until morning, after a woman—I guess she was a bag lady, but nice—said not to worry, she'd look out for me (which felt OK and not scary like it should have). And she DID stay with me, but she was gone when I woke up, and there was this white feather where she'd been sitting, so I took it. There was a train at 7:00 a.m., and I'm on it writing this. It's like talking to myself, only people don't think you're crazy when you're just writing. I'm beginning to see why people used to write journals a lot. It's like tweeting all the time.

10:00 a.m., Castle Cary Station

Now I'm here sitting on a bench in a station in Somerset. The train manager said I have to take a bus to get to Mount, and then I guess I'll just walk—even though I'm pretty tired now AND it's raining.

11:00 a.m., bus shelter by the side of the road.

Oh—they're everywhere! Like flies. They're swarming. And pushing me! If I follow them, I have a feeling they'll take me right to the Hall. I hope someone's there. Or maybe not. Maybe this isn't a good idea. Maybe I should just go to Nebraska. I could call Mom.

OMG! I just pressed the whole swarm of them. I could hear them sort of squealing in the book, but they all flew away when I opened it. I'm beginning to see different types. They're really kind of cute, even when they're pressed.

5:00 p.m.

Well, I'm here. It took longer than I thought it would, and just walking up the drive took forever. It felt like it was miles long, but maybe that was because I kept seeing the house looming up at the end of the drive and for such a long time it didn't seem any closer and then all of a sudden it was right there – or, I guess, I was right there. It's like a manor house in an old movie.

Even though the Hall is one big ruin and it looks like one wing burned down, it's a beautiful ruin, all romantic and Gothic-y, made with warm gold-colored stone walls. Where the roof is still on, it's all slopey and there are a lot of chimneys. There's still glass in some of the windows and it's all little panes in diamond shapes and the whole thing looks like a fairy-tale house, with a big woodland growing almost right up to the left side of it, overgrown lawns, and an obelisk on the right. When I arrived at the huge front door, it was standing open, like I was expected. Instead of seeming sinister, it felt like coming Home. Not to a home I've ever lived in, but to my capital "H" Home. I'm Home. I've looked around a little bit. There are some rooms still usable, but I don't know if anyone lives here at all—I haven't seen anyone yet. I'm glad I saved some sandwiches from the train.

8:00 p.m.

There's no phone, and I can't get a signal for my cell either. The electricity isn't working, as far as I can tell. There are switches and wall sockets and a few lightbulbs still in place, but nothing comes on. I have a little flashlight, but that's it. Maybe tomorrow I can find the fuse box and fuses and see if I can try to get some lights to work.

There <u>are</u> LIGHTS, though—the little floating lights. It's the fairies! They glow! When they gather together in a bunch, I can see by the light. I don't feel so alone with them here. I followed them around, and they led me to a sofa and some cushions and a blanket in one of the rooms. They're helping me! I'm so tired—I think I can sleep.

June 6, 9:00 a.m.

It's not SO much a ruin. There are rooms and stairs and walls with old-fashioned wallpaper, and some places still have ceilings too, with plasterwork in complicated designs. There's still furniture in some of the rooms and paintings on the walls. It's beautiful. I love it. I found a fuse box in the kitchen and some old fuses. At least some of the lights work now. I can see the little fairies, but they don't glow when there's daylight. I should be afraid, shouldn't I? It's like one of those houses in a really scary film, but I'm NOT scared, at all. And I wasn't scared last night. I dreamed about the fairies, and there was music in the dream and some sheep and maybe a llama. Weird. Mom and Dad must be looking for me.

This morning when I came to the kitchen, there was food laid out, with a white feather on the table too. Strange—it's like the ones I was given in London. There's GOT to be someone living here somewhere. They put out bread and butter and honey and milk. It's really good. It's kind of like "Beauty and the Beast," where servants are invisible. I hope there's not a Beast (well, unless he's really a prince—LOL).

I feel like the house LIKES me—the house and the woods along the side of the house too. I can see them from the window in my room. They're beautiful. I've never seen woods like this before. SO old and the trees are SO big. The little fairies disappear into the woods sometimes. I want to follow and see where they go, but not yet. Rain. Rain. Rain. Rain. Rain. Rain.

COTTINGTON ARCHIVE

COTTINGTON ARCHIVE
COTTINGTON ARCHIVE

Found a whole bunch of archive stickers — and they're still sticky!

June 7, 11:00 a.m.

I've found something amazing! It's a whole room with a light in it that still works! I went up some really steep stairs, and there it was. It's an archive room (I know that because it says so on the door—duh), but it's really more like an old junk room. It's FULL of Cottington stuff: books and papers and clothes and even some armor and really, really strange bits of machines and things.

Noon.

OK, I just had THE MOST TRAUMATIC EXPERIENCE EVER!!!!! One of those weird machine things ATE MY HAIR!!!! I was bending down to look at it and I only just touched it and it started to make this grinding noise and then it kind of pulled my hair into a gear on the side—a whole BIG strand of it! I couldn't get it out. I had to cut it off—thank God there are scissors here! I had to cut the rest of my hair to match. Actually, I like it, I guess. The machine thing seems to be working all by itself now. It's whirring away. Maybe it needed to eat hair to get going. Ha! Maybe it needed MY hair. That's kind of creepy. I hope it doesn't need anything else.

There are stuffed badgers and a skink (or maybe it's a newt) There's also an old typewriter and a stack of paper! I think I might use that from now on. My hand gets so tired writing like this, but I like writing about everything, even if it's like talking to myself. I can just stick the pages into my journal as I type them. I wish there was more light—the fairies won't keep still in one place long enough for me to see anything clearly enough, and the light bulb is really dim. I grabbed a notebook and some photos and took them back to "my" room. That's where I am now. I made a nest for myself on an old daybed in the corner of the room. There are lots of pillows and velvet covers, and it's pretty lush and exotic. And it doesn't smell like mice or mold—it smells like honey and lavender. I found matches and a whole box of candles—beeswax. The smell is fabulous!

Wow, now THIS is amazing!!!

I found a sort of notebook/sketchbook by Angelica's brother, Quentin (she never mentioned her brother in the books!). It's falling apart, so I'm going to stick the loose pages in MY journal to keep them. This is SO cool. He was an inventor, I guess. And a soldier in WWI, and he had shell shock and went kind of crazy and "saw things" (well, he IS a Cottington!). And some of Angelica's writing and "pressings" are in it too. She is SO funny (and I don't think she means to be either)! They write to each other instead of talking—how bizarre—and they call each other Jelly and Tinny (that's for Angelica and Quentin—I worked that out!). And fairies! Pressed on the pages (they still look squashed to me) just like in the books I found in Camden, but for real! Jelly is truly weird, but I don't think Tinny is—maybe just eccentric. I pressed some more fairies to see if it would be different here. They still don't seem to mind, and then I get to see them—but I'd like to see them better without having to squash them. Maybe I can make something to capture them—like one of Quentin's inventions. I LOVE his diagrams! SO cool! All about how to capture the essence of stains and see what they look like—like they might be fairies or something. I'm going to try to get one of them to work again. Maybe that "Learning How to Make Useful Things in Case of Disaster" course I took in school will come in handy after all. Glad I paid attention!

Quentin's desk

What IS this stuff?

Found lots of little cards
on Quentin's desk

Don't know what they mean,
but they're kind of cool.

Jelly 1902 – "a fine catch".

June 10, 1919, 8:00 a.m.

Jinny, my voice has gone! It has completely disappeared, and when I open my mouth nothing comes out but a squeak! If we are to communicate at all today, I'll have to write notes. I'll expect you to respond in kind, just to be fair. We can use my journal, and that way I can press at the same time! I'd hate to miss any of them. I'll have Hazlett deliver this to you immediately.

Your loving Jelly.

Hold still — Got you!

June 10, 1919, 9:00 am.

Ok, old girl~if you insist, Must make a quick dash down to the kitchen. Cook's noticed a peculiar stain leaking out from behind the cupboard. I say, hope it isn't Ruffles. Haven't seen him since he chased that mouse into the pantry on Tuesday. No, Cook would have heard him whining, surely. Do come down and have a look, J.

Your Tinny.

June 10, 1919, 11:00 a.m.

Tinny you absolute toad!!!! You knew that was my tipsy cake. Cook baked it especially for me. She won't make another one now. I just know she won't. Oh, I do hate you Tinny. REALLY I do. Why can't you just go away again? It was SO perfect whilst you were away. I don't care if it was muddy and horrible in the trenches. I don't care. Cook made that tipsy cake for me~well, for them, really. They love tipsy cake, as you well know, I was certain to get some perfect pressings when they came to eat it. And now you've ruined it.

You toad.

xxx, Jelly.

What's Tipsy Cake?

Sounds good though ~ wish I had some!

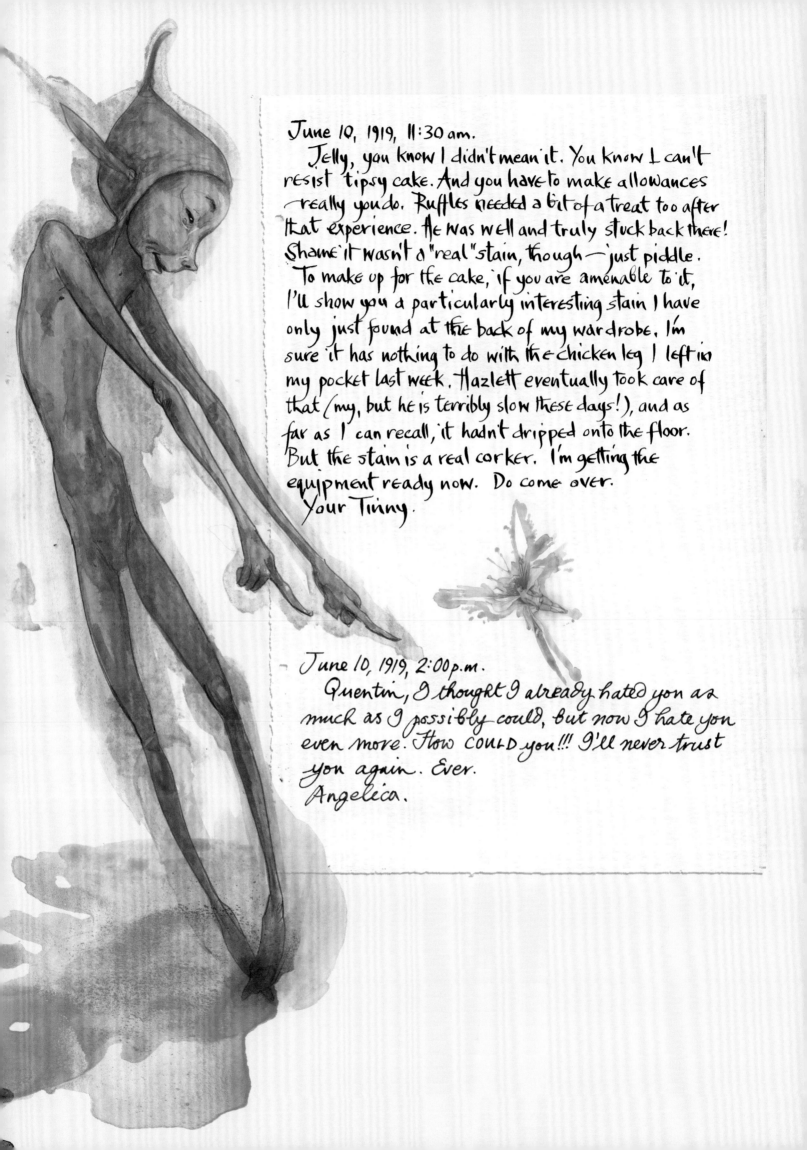

June 10, 1919, 11:30 am.

Jelly, you know I didn't mean it. You know I can't resist tipsy cake. And you have to make allowances really you do. Ruffles needed a bit of a treat too after that experience. He was well and truly stuck back there! Shame it wasn't a "real" stain, though—just piddle.

To make up for the cake, if you are amenable to it, I'll show you a particularly interesting stain I have only just found at the back of my wardrobe. I'm sure it has nothing to do with the chicken leg I left in my pocket last week. Hazlett eventually took care of that (my, but he is terribly slow these days!), and as far as I can recall, it hadn't dripped onto the floor. But the stain is a real corker. I'm getting the equipment ready now. Do come over.
Your Tinny.

June 10, 1919, 2:00 p.m.

Quentin, I thought I already hated you as much as I possibly could, but now I hate you even more. How COULD you!!! I'll never trust you again. Ever.
Angelica.

June 10, 1919, 3:00 p.m.

Jelly,— your face!!! What a spectacle you made of yourself! It's a good thing Hazlett wasn't around to see it. By the way, I got the Sniffer working again; just a few minor adjustments— I added a sock and some semolina to the inner chamber— and it ticks over as good as gold now. Might I come over to your wing and have a go in the little tower room? I'll let you look for fairies over here, if you like. They MUST know by now that your wing of the house is terribly incommodious, with all the slamming and pressing and snapping constantly going on. At least I don't press them. Fairies don't seem to mind being sniffed or licked—but it's hard to tell. DO let me come over. I'll wait in the hall. I won't come if you don't want me too.

Your Tinny.

June 10, 5:00 p.m

Well, I say, Jelly, that's not very sporting of you. Barricading the hall just isn't on old girl. Your whole wing of the house reeks of fairy stains and smells, and it isn't fair if you won't let me come over to test them. I'm a scientist, don't you know! This is important work you're stopping, and truly I can't allow it. I'm vexed, Jelly. Really I am. I'll tell Cook to never listen to you again, and you'll not get anything else to tempt them unless you go into the village and visit the vicarage for tea. I know you hate going there, but you'll have no choice if you want cake.
T.

Remember me.

June 10, 10:00pm.

Dinner in silence. How I enjoyed that! There is nothing you can possibly say that I would want to hear, and certainly not whilst eating Brown Windsor soup. Do you remember when we were little and Miss Allenby made us sit through every meal without talking? Well, we couldn't talk because she made us chew the soup, remember? "Fletcherize, my dears, fletcherize," she always said. It was so difficult then, but now I do believe it to be the answer. Not fletcherizing—I mean NOT speaking! If we must meet, we will communicate only by writing, even when my voice returns. Today has been a revelation. I may never speak to you again!

Damn! Look at that—just as I was about to finish as well. Give this back when you've read it, will you, Jinny? It's a good pressing. The little thing landed right on the middle of the paper. I've not had one like that in simply ages. And they DON'T mind being pressed, you know. They adore the attention, the silly things!

x x x
Jelly.

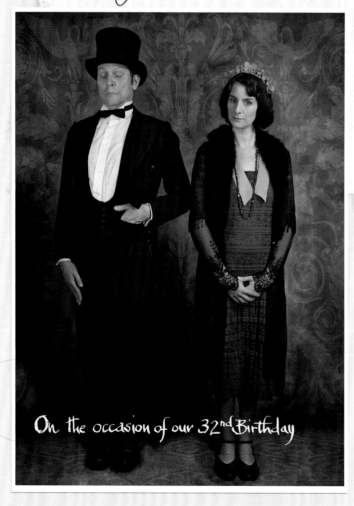

On the occasion of our 32nd Birthday

June 11, 9:00 a.m.

I say, old girl, I've just had the oddest dream ever. I was back in the trenches again — no surprise there; my dreams are almost always about that — but this time it was different. I was watching the remnants of the dead trees (they always reminded me of ghouls, with their ghastly black branches reaching out for me like giant fingers) in no man's land and thinking about what we would be doing next, when all of a sudden I saw three figures standing right out there in the middle of the mud near the blackened trees. They looked, for all the world, like archers of some sort — not the kind you would see practicing on the targets here, but very old-fashioned ones, almost like something from that book about the Middle Ages we read in the nursery library. They stood there looking at me, and then they turned toward the Germans and took aim and shot arrows right into their trenches. When they turned away, I could see wings, or something rather like them, at their backs — or maybe there just streaks of light. I'm not too clear on that. In my dream all the time I saw them I felt safe, you know? I never felt safe in the trenches, but at that moment I did. Funny isn't it? I'm sure I've seen them before. I want to feel safe like that again, Jelly. I know I'm home, but it doesn't seem to matter: I still don't feel safe. I hope I dream about them again.

Your Tinny

COTTINGTON ARCHIVE

June 11, 10:30 a.m

Oh, Jinny, you poor, dear darling. I wish I could make it all go away. I had a funny dream about two bunnies dancing a tango in the garden, but it wasn't a SPECIAL dream like yours. Sometimes I dream about the strange man we used to see at the edge of the woods before the war. Do you remember him, and the rest of them? I dream about them often, but they never make me feel safe at all and none of them have wings. Sometimes I wonder if either of us knows what safe is. I don't think I've ever felt particularly safe in this house, but I imagine to you it must feel like paradise after the trenches and all that. I'd guard you with a bow and arrow if you wanted me to, but then I might shoot you by mistake. I wouldn't mean to, you know that, but I'm not a very good shot. Oh, Jinny do be careful. I'm not sure what I mean by that, but just DO be careful.

Your Jelly.

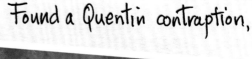

Found a Quentin contraption,

5:00 p.m.

I've been hiding in the archive room because the police (I THINK they were police) were here looking for me! They shouted and tramped around the garden and grounds, and then they came into the house. I could tell they didn't think there was anyone here, and they gave up pretty quickly. One of them actually got really close to where I was. When he opened the archive room door, I could swear he looked straight at me, but he didn't see me! The fairies seemed particularly thick then. It's like the fairies don't want me to be found. I can tell. They're helping me. They want me to stay here.

7:00 p.m.

I made this fairy-catching book out of my phone and some stuff that was lying around here. I'm glad my printer runs on batteries too, because the wall sockets here are really old-fashioned and my plug doesn't fit, but now it prints out photos and what I catch in my book AND I can print on leaves as well as paper! I'm going to try fixing some of Quentin's contraptions. I bet I can get them to work. I've looked at them enough times that they're beginning to make sense to me. I can "feel" how they should work—like I can see into his mind. I think it has something to do with quantum physics, making sense of things you can't see or can't explain. There's a lot going on here that I can't explain, that's for sure! Glad I got A's in math and science last year! My brain hurts when I think about all this, but I just realized I'm not getting headaches anymore.

I wonder if I can get it to work.......... and if I do, what's it going to do?

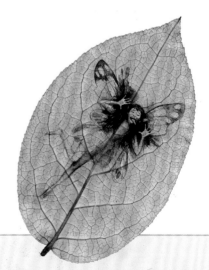

All these clothes! My phone takes such crazy pictures now
that I've attached it to this machine thing! I'm a Lady! I'm
Lady Madeline Cottington.

Look at me!!! I'm Mad Maddi C.—I'm a Cottington and I'm a
fearless fairy hunter!

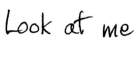

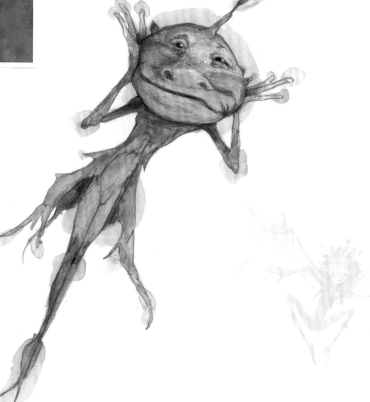

-ook at me

I'm a FAIRY!

FAERIES

Flora Cottington, 1877, in her 65th year.

Oh, Euphemia, my own, my dearest grandchild,
    They would take me from you and confine me in a space so very small that I might no longer take flight and soar with my heart's friends. I pray I should grow to be so tiny, I would slip beneath the door of my chamber and fly away. I pray I should grow to be so large, I would burst through the walls that hold me here and fly away. Fly or no, I must leave you, my own dearest, and seek refuge in the woods. If they find me and bind me and take me away, remember that I love you always. Remember the songs and the stories. They are true—all true: the singing and the ringing of the tiny bells. I hear them calling me, and I shall dance on young feet again. I shall dance away until the ferns enclose and hide me, the flowers drown me in their scent, the trees embrace me, hold me safe within their leafy arms, and I shall vanish. Remember me, my dearest, and hold me in your heart as I hold you in mine.

In haste,
Your loving grandmama, Flora,
Lady Cottington

I found this letter today from an ancestor named Flora, and so it seems that we Cottingtons have always been "different" and the woods have always been important to us.

The letter's so sad and beautiful—though, granted, slightly insane. I wonder if she ever came out of the woods. Somehow I don't think so. But maybe that's OK too.

"Flora" must be a family name from way back. Why was the family always trying to stop them—the ones who saw things, that is? Just like my dad. I guess there are the Cottingtons who believe and the Cottingtons who think the other ones are crazy. Well, I know which side I'M on.

June 8, 6:00 a.m.—I NEVER get up this early!
Wow! Quentin was amazing. I keep digging around in the
archive room, and there's just SO much down here. There are
lots of boxes stamped with the symbol of a beehive with
bees flying around it. I looked over the main door, and
it's the same symbol there too. I guess it must be the
Cottington coat of arms or something. But it's funny,
because when you look really, REALLY closely, they're NOT
all bees. Some of them are fairies (of course!), but they're
all mostly worn away. So the Cottingtons always knew about
fairies—not just Angelica and Quentin and Euphemia and
Flora (poor Flora), but way, way back to Sir Somebody-
Somebody Cottington who came back from the Crusades (like
my dad said). He built this house, and he built something
else on the grounds too. I can't figure out what it is or
where it is, but it has to do with bees, I'm pretty sure.
Maybe the Cottingtons were beekeepers—or fairy keepers. Can
you get fairy honey???

It's here in Quentin's diary. The beehive hut. It's in the woods somewhere, and I've got to find it, because it's important. I think maybe you're meant to stand in the beehive hut or pray in there or something. I'm sure it's all in Quentin's diary.

1919

At least now, I know what I'm looking for.

There's a generator here—kind of. I'm sure it's one of Quentin's contraptions, and it looks like it might work if I can figure it out. If that old fuse box fails, this might come in handy. I hope it generates electricity and not something weird!

June 12, 11:00 am.
Thank you, Jinny.
   You see? It's better when we don't speak.
I do wish you hadn't tried to lick the pressing,
though. I know it was fresh, but now it's not
quite the same. It isn't as bright as it was, and
I think you licked the best of it right off the
page. I might let you come over to my wing
today if you promise to NOT talk to me or do
anything horrible or use ANY of my notebooks
OR stay too long OR lick anything.
XXX
Jelly.

June 13, 9:00 p.m.

I say, Jelly, what a cracking day! Thanks for letting me come over, old thing. The little tower room was absolutely crammed with smells, and the stain under the bed was first-rate. Had you seen it before? It looks like it might be a lingerer. I'll have to come over again in a few days and see if it's still there. You won't mind will you? I'll let you have a go in the west wing library. I know they're thick around the window. You know the one I mean? Overlooking the woods? They love that window. Just like flies in summer, except they don't die along the sill - they pick themselves up and fly away. I've tried opening the window for them, but they don't seem to want to fly out. They just enjoy throwing themselves against it, rather like when you press them. Strange. I don't like the noise they make. It reminds me too much of the guns. I wish they'd stop.

Your Tinny

A typical day in the garden.

October 19, 9:00 a.m.

No dreams last night. Thank goodness for that. I woke up feeling tip-top. I think I'll venture into the woods today, Jelly. Would you like to come out with me? I'm getting the equipment ready now. I'll take the mechanical Sniffer and maybe the new Steam-Powered Left-Handed Stain Locator and we'll see what we can find. I've been looking through the archive room and came across an absolutely ripping design for a beehive-shaped structure built of stone. It appears to be the plans for something built on the grounds here at the Hall. Hard to tell—the parchment is terribly old. I have the feeling that it's that funny hut thing near the edge of the woods. You know the one I mean? Looks like a huge beehive, or it might if it were uncovered a bit—masses of ivy everywhere! I've seen the little ones buzzing around it like bees. Ha! They seem fascinated by the shape, but at the same time I feel as though they're trying to keep us away. Well, they're not going to stop me. Let's explore, Jelly. Do say you'll come out.

Your Tinny.

October 19, 6:00 p.m.

What a day! How did you know that today would be so perfect to venture out near the woods? I hardly ever go there (as you well know), but today they seemed so welcoming. And the little ones—well, what a terrific catch that was! So many of them, all hovering around the outside of that funny hut. When we were little, I just thought of it as a dull stone garden shed I can't even remember seeing it clearly before. I wonder if Abbott has chopped away the ivy.

Did you hear the singing? I heard it so clearly. Didn't like it much, though. It reminded me of something, but I can't for the life of me think what it was. It made me all nervy and rather itchy, like I had a ferret in my bloomers. But then they came in absolute droves, and as soon as I started pressing away, I felt myself again. Funny, isn't it?
xxx
Jelly.

October 19, 9:00 p.m.

I'll send this over with Hazlett in the morning, Jelly. I just want to write it while it's still fresh in the old noggin.

I did hear the singing. I've heard it before too — quite a few times actually — but funnily enough, hearing it made me recall the music in that dream I told you about, the one with those archer fellows. They were singing, or maybe there was singing around them, but it was the same tune, I'm sure of that. What does it mean, Jelly? It's all a bit too confusing for my poor old noodle! I want to go back to the little hut and have a good poke around at the walls inside. I could smell them even from the doorway, and I'm quite positive that what I saw wasn't just mildew. No, I'm certain it was more than that. I must know. I must find out why they cluster there.

I'm going to ask something of you now, Jelly, and I don't want you taking offence, old girl. Will you please NOT come with me again? I can't have you frightening them away with your cries of "tally ho!!!" and your infernal smashing and blundering about. I know you can't help yourself, but sometimes you are the most appallingly clumsy woman when it comes to stealth. How you ever manage to catch anything I have no idea. I must have quiet and a bit of peace to study the walls and the stains. I don't know why I'm so drawn to that hut, but I am. I think I might find an answer there. I'm not quite sure what the question is, but there's something missing in me. It's been missing for a long time — since before the war. Maybe it's always been missing and I'm just now realising it. Do try to understand, Jelly.

I'll let you have the run of the west wing while I'm out.
In hope,
    Your Tinny

October 20, 9:00 am.

Oh, that IS selfish, you absolute beast. It's not fair to keep them to yourself, and all for those silly stains. AND if you're missing something, I could help you find it. I know I could. AND how dare you say I'm clumsy! How dare you! You have no idea how stealthy I can be. And as for having the run of the west wing, I'll have you know that whilst you were away, I HAD the run of it EVERY DAY and I ran AND I skipped AND maybe even turned a cartwheel or two. Sometimes I took my skirt and petticoats off and ran through the house in my bloomers with no shoes or stockings on either. Hazlett was terribly shocked when he came upon me in the long gallery! He took to wearing a blindfold when he knew I was running about in less than he felt was appropriate. Poor old Hazlett; he's really much more suited to being a vicar than a butler.

You are SO selfish, Jinny. I'll go where I please. So there.

xxx

J.

October 20, 4:00 p.m.

WELL, that's torn it. I wish you hadn't felt the need to follow me to the hut, Jelly. Why couldn't you let them be? Just this once I really needed you not to blunder in and start smashing at all and sundry with that damn book of yours. It felt bad. It felt wrong, and you wouldn't stop. They were coming to me and I could hear that music again and suddenly I knew where it was coming from and I knew I could find it and maybe even find more than just the singing. What have you done? I have a terrible feeling about this. They aren't happy. I don't mean the little ones. It doesn't much matter if they're happy or not, but the others? That matters. There seem to be quite a few of them all gathered around the hut. They're far too grand to vex, but you've more than vexed them today. What are we going to do now? I know you can't help it, old girl, but I'm quite certain we're in a bit of a mess. I could see their eyes as they watched you smashing away. They weren't at ALL happy. I'm afraid we're in for a bit of a rough time if we ever go back there. And I HAVE to go back, Jelly, really I do.

Your Tinny

October 20, 6:00 p.m.

    I'm sure I don't know what you mean! It was much the same as always, Jinny. I collected some absolutely lovely pressings out there (PRESSINGS, NOT smashings — I wish you wouldn't refer to my collecting in that way). That hut really does seem to attract them. I didn't see anything apart from the little ones. Did you mean you saw something like those people we used to see? I wouldn't bother with them or anyone else in the woods. After all, the woods belong to us! They are the Cottington Woods, and I'll do as I please in them—or at the edge of them. I don't think I'll venture as far as the hut again for a while. NOT because I'm frightened. I'm certainly NOT frightened! I just do not WISH to. I shall stick to the house and the gardens. There are absolute masses of little ones to be caught, and I shan't need to look farther than that. You carry on. I'm sure they'll forgive you (whoever they are) and make allowances because of what you've been through and all that. I know I have to. And I didn't hear the singing. Well, if I did, it sounded more like buzzing to me, and when I heard it, it made me quite giddy for a moment. I don't like that hut, Jinny. I wish you didn't find it so fascinating. It's dirty and old, and I'm sure it must be damp and mouldy inside. Don't go back there. Please don't.

Your loving sister,
Jelly

October 31, — a.m.

   I'm writing in haste, Jelly. I'm going back. I can't leave it any longer and I can't stop myself. I've tried this past week or so, but I'm dreaming so much again and every dream has them in it and I can see them every time I shut my eyes. I must do this. I'm going to go right through the hut and out the other little door opposite now that the ivy is gone. I went last night while you were sleeping (don't deny it — I could hear you snoring as I passed the door) and walked all around the hut. So odd, but it seemed to take me hours and hours. There's nothing special about the outside, apart from the constant flutter of the little ones, but when I went in and looked through the door at the back, it was different somehow. I'm not sure what I mean by this, but I knew if I walked through the door, I'd be somewhere else. Does that make sense, Jelly? Probably not. It doesn't matter. I'm going. I WILL come back. Once I've found whatever it is, perhaps I'll be able to rest a bit. Whatever happens, I'm sure to collect some absolutely cracking stains!

   Your Tinny

   P.S. Please don't go anywhere near the hut. It won't be for you. Of that I'm quite positive.

November 1, — a.m.

Oh, Jinny. Oh dear. I don't quite know what to do now. You did it on purpose, didn't you? Choosing the only day I was out of the house. I had no choice. The vicar arranged the tea such a long time ago, and I HAD promised. He asked about you, and I told him that you were better EVERY day. Did I lie, Jinny? ARE you better? I fear not. I know you said not to, but I'll wait by the hut for you. I'm not going to go in, though. I'll never go in.

I just realized that I'm writing this to myself. Please, please come home. I'll be extra kind to you. I brought you a piece of cake from the vicarage. It will go stale if you're not home to eat it soon. Oh never mind. It's gone now.

6:00 p.m.—It's not raining! YAY!

I found the beehive hut. It's really overgrown with vines and brambles, but I can tell that it's there. The little fairies are driving me crazy today. They were buzzing around my head the whole time I was looking for the hut, and when I found it they just went wild trying to get me to leave (I think). They even pinched me! I caught some of them in my book, but they still wouldn't stop. But—and this is kind of scary—I heard something coming from inside the hut: whispers. MY name. Someone whispered my name. Somebody wants me to go in there, even if the little ones don't (just realized that's what Angelica called them too!). It's really late already. I went out early this morning, and now it's evening. Twelve hours—I can't remember being near the hut that long at all. Funny. Scary. That's what happened to Quentin.

There's food in the kitchen again.

6:00 a.m.—Again! SO early!

Maybe I'll get the hut cleared today so I can go inside. I HAVE to see what's in there. There's a bee carved over the doorway—I can see that already.

There's so much of Quentin's notebook missing. I'm going to see if there are more pages lying around in the archive room. I can't quite make out what he's talking about—something about a "mark" on all of the Cottingtons in the past. What does that mean? A birthmark? He was SO into stains and smells and weird things like that—more than just SEEING the fairies or pressing them like jelly. Why would you want to smell them? Or lick the stains they leave?

10:00 a.m.

There IS more—just loose pages, but I can figure out most of the order. Oh, this page is earlier. It's beautiful—like angels with bows and arrows.

And here he says he's seen them again! At the hut, maybe? Kind of vague. He calls them "the others"—not the little ones. I feel sorry for him. He seems so lost.

November 1, 1921, 4:00 p.m.

No, I will damn well NOT speak to you! I can't
bring myself to speak to you. I'll write and that's
that. This isn't funny, Jinny. I DON'T understand
and I DON'T think you're being at all nice. I thought
you were dead. I thought you had gone away just
like, well, you KNOW who, and that I'd never see
again. And now you're here and pretending that
nothing happened. Two years happened, Jinny!
Two whole years, and you say you don't remember?
How can that be? It hasn't been just a day and a
night. I don't care how often you insist that's true.
It has been TWO whole years, and I can't stand
to have you deny it. Really I can't.

Jelly.

November 1, 1921, 6:00 p.m
   I don't know what more to say. I've NOT been away
two years, old girl. I can't have done. Just not possible.
I mean, give a fellow some credit ~ I'd know, don't you think?
I'd have to know wouldn't I?

Remember Your Tinny

OMG—he WAS lost. He went through the hut and was away for two years!!!! How spooky is that? She's SO mad at him—but it's so sad. I'm not going to go in after all. Jelly wouldn't go in. Maybe she's not as crazy as I thought.

No—there's GOT to be a way in and out that's safe.

November 1, 1921, 7:00 p.m.

I asked Hazlett—well, I had to shout, actually (good lord, he's deaf!)—and he said that it IS 1921 and I HAVE been away that long. He says it isn't his place to question where I've been, but he did say how sad you were without me. No pressings? No tipsy cake? The frightening thing, Jelly, is that if I HAVE been gone that long, I truly don't remember a thing. I know I went through the door at the back of the hut. I remember that. Then I remember wandering around a bit. I had thought that when I went through the door, I would come out somewhere else—I remember telling you that—but it didn't seem very different to me. Not really. I think I wandered all night, but it couldn't have been night, because it never got past twilight. I followed a path of sorts, and no matter how long I walked, I ended up back in front of that door in the hut. I finally just gave up and came through again, but only after I stayed in the hut for a little while. I suppose it was to collect that stain I saw on the wall. Strange—I just can't remember. I'm feeling dis-combobulated, Jelly. I think I might be ill. Or maybe not ill. Maybe I feel better than I did. I'm not altogether sure. I wonder if I'll dream tonight. I'm rather afraid to sleep, you know. I'm not sure I can stand more nights of them looking at me. If I call out in the night, will you come to me? Please come like you used to, when we were small and you'd hold my hand whenever I was frightened. I'm frightened now, Jelly, and I don't know why.

Your Tinny

COTTINGTON ARCHIVE

November 1, 1921, 9:00 pm.

I'm here, Jinny. Your Jelly is here and I'll hold your hand and everything will be fine again. They won't come near you. I won't let them. I love you, Jinny. Even when I hate you, I love you.

XXX

J.

4:00 p.m.

I think they're here for me. The "others"—Quentin's "others."
I've seen the fairy man again and an old couple. It's really
weird, but they look a lot like the cab driver and the old
bag lady in the train station. Maybe they're fairies and
were there to guide me. If they're here, I think they must
be the ones leaving food out for me too. That's why there's a
white feather on the kitchen table. They must want me here,
but why won't they talk to me?

6:00 p.m.

I'm SOOO tired of bread and honey and milk. It's nice that
they're there, but I'd die for a hamburger and fries right
now. Maybe not die—maybe not.

I heard someone shouting to me. I think it was Dad,
but I'm not sure, and I didn't answer. I don't think he'd
recognize me now even if he did see me. Mad Maddi. Let him
worry. He's NOT going to lock me up in Tonawanda with Aunt
Tilly! It's kind of strange, but I feel like if Dad WANTED
to find me, he could. Why do I get the feeling he WANTS me
here? I'm crazy.

Next day
I dreamed about them—bees and fairies. I think it was a
nice dream, but I can't remember now. I saw the others too.
They were calling to me—smiling and beckoning. They
wanted me to come with them into the woods—and NOT
through the beehive hut. They wanted me to come straight
in and be with them. "Always"—that's the word I kept
hearing, or maybe "all ways." I hope it was a dream.

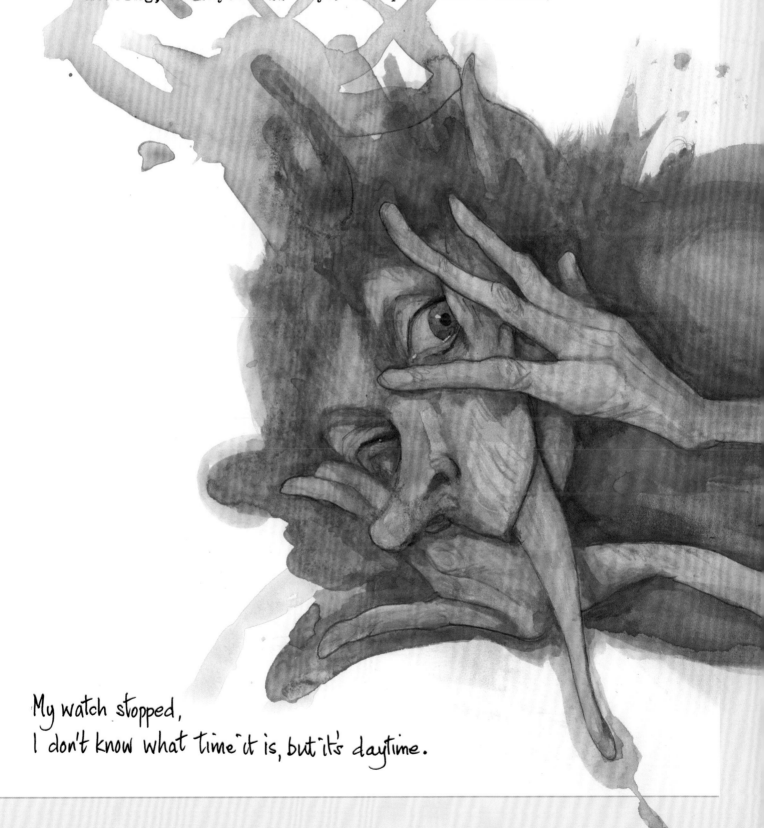

My watch stopped,
I don't know what time it is, but it's daytime.

I'm in the archives. It's a tattoo! That's the Cottingtons'
"mark." It's a tattoo of a bee. There are all these drawings
of ancient Cottingtons with the bee tattoo on their arm.
It's a key. It's got to be a key. Quentin says something
about it here.

Well, J., I think I've solved it! The Cottington ancestors all tattooed one of their arms with an image of a bee! Darned if I know exactly why, but I'll bet you a tipsy cake it's got to do with getting to the otherworld and back safely. It's the only reason a Cottington would stoop to something as outré as a tattoo! If I take a bit of the essence I collected from that fresh pressing of yours and mix it with honey and blackberries, I think I'll have the right sort of ink for a tattoo on my left arm, because then I could do it myself. I KNOW you'd do it for me, J., but I think perhaps not, old thing. You haven't the most delicate of touches, you know! Wish me luck!

Your Tinny

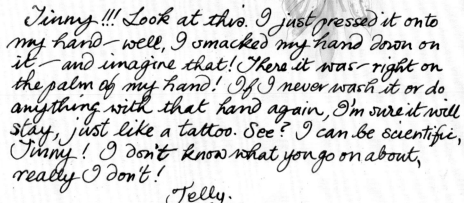

Tinny!!! Look at this. I just pressed it onto my hand—well, I smacked my hand down on it—and imagine that! There it was—right on the palm of my hand! If I never wash it or do anything with that hand again, I'm sure it will stay, just like a tattoo. See? I can be scientific, Tinny! I don't know what you go on about, really I don't!

Jelly.

Later
I found the plan for the hut. It IS old—1298. Wow. I think
the first Lord Cottington drew this and then had it built
here. It's got to be the same hut.

Later later
I cleared the rest of the ivy away, and it's all uncovered now. I went in and looked around. It's a dome inside. It's just big enough to stand up in, and I can touch the walls all around if I stretch out my arms. I've seen pictures of buildings like this in Greece and Ireland and lots of other countries too. They're mysterious, and nobody seems to know exactly what they were used for. They're beautiful. IT'S beautiful. There's a door in the opposite side, but as far as I can tell it just opens into the woods. There isn't anywhere else for it to go. I opened the door a crack and looked out, but somehow I just couldn't make myself step through it. I will, though. I saw the strange couple again by the edge of the woods, but before I could call out to them, they just seemed to melt into the trees. Somehow I can't imagine I'll get a photo either.

Lots later

I think it must be late, because it's dark now. I don't
remember seeing the sunset. I'm back in the archives, and
it's really strange, but I think the stuff has shifted
around. There are more things that I haven't seen before.
There are more diary pages from Quentin too. They are
under one of the stuffed badgers. I feel better in my
armor—safer. I pressed a few little ones again just to see
what would happen. It's kind of horrible, but I can't seem
to stop myself. I feel like I have to go on pressing. I've
got a real knack for it! And besides, the little ones seem
to like it!

Morning again
Another weird dream. I grew wings! I could feel them
coming out of my back, and I could move them a bit—not fly
exactly, but open and close them. It felt amazing,
actually. Then I dreamed I saw the fairy man again, and he
opened his arms to me like I should walk right into them.
I wanted to.

A little later
Now that the generator's working, I tried to find a socket
on the side of it or some way to charge my phone. While I
was looking, I laid the phone on top of it—and it's
charging! Just by itself! Now I can take more photos and
not worry. I put my watch on it too, and now it's going
again—but backward, and it's kind of sticky.

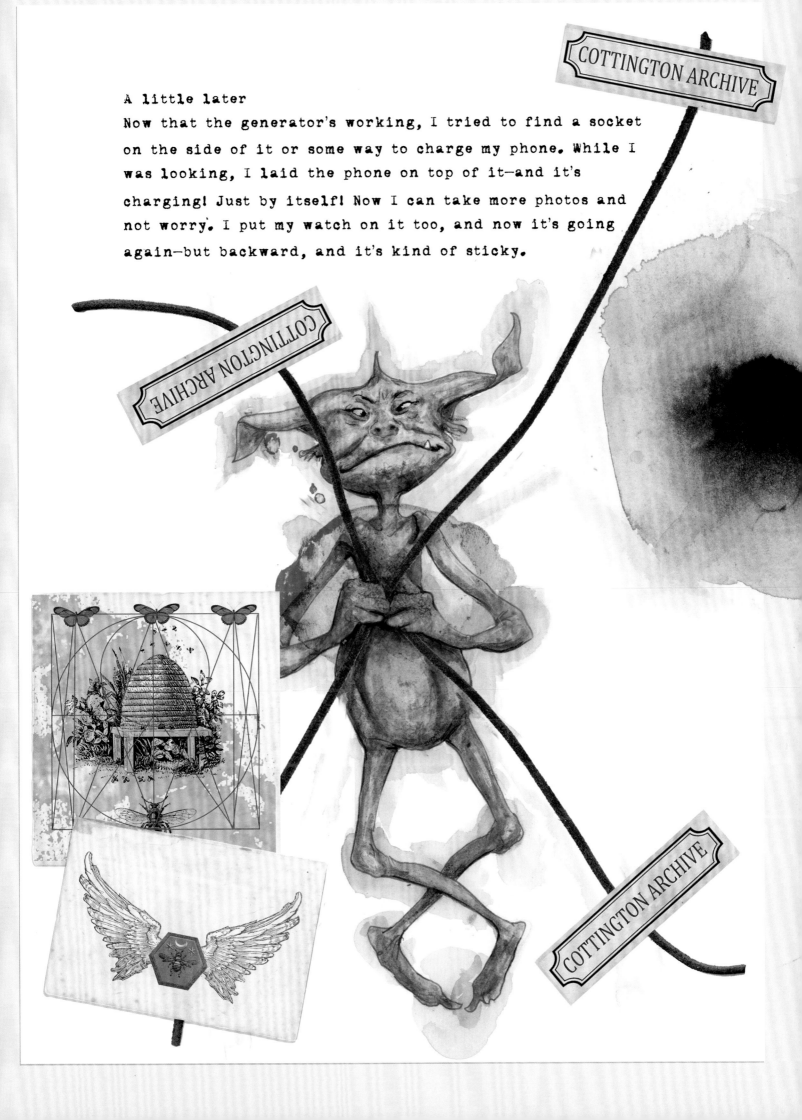

COTTINGTON ARCHIVE

COTTINGTON ARCHIVE

COTTINGTON ARCHIVE

Cottington Hall 1974

Later later

I put on my armor again and explored more of the house—
well, the parts that are still standing. It's not THAT
ruined—or maybe I'm getting used to it. I follow the little
ones, and they seem to want to show me things. I think I
might have found Angelica's room or somebody's since then.
I found a little drawing in a drawer of the desk signed,
"From Flora to Rupert—1974." It's of a kind of house on
wheels, standing on a big lawn (the lawn outside the Hall
probably looked like this at one time). It's funny—kind of
like a gypsy caravan or Baba Yaga's hut on chicken feet.
On the back it says, "We are the travelers between night
and day and moon and sun and here and there." The really
weird thing is that my aunt and father are named Flora
and Rupert. But this can't be them, because I worked it out
and they'd have been twenty-two and twenty-four in 1974
and they were in America long before then. Weren't they? It
can't be them. I took the drawing back down with me—I
didn't want to stay in there.

But what if they WERE here then, Flora and Dad? Just
like Angelica and Quentin. What if they didn't leave until
they were grown up? Dad never REALLY said. He would
never talk about it at all. Maybe Mom and I just assumed he
was a child when he left. Or maybe everybody knows but me.
What a lunatic family. But why would they leave here? I
feel like I'll NEVER want to leave, and I just got here. I
kind of feel like I CAN'T leave.

I'm going to read more of Quentin's diary. I wish
Angelica hadn't spoiled so much of it with her pressings!!!
But they loved each other, Jelly and Tinny. They really
did.

What ho, J.!

Back and forth, in and out, just like one of those spiffing revolving doors at Selfridges! And no time lost! It's easy when you know how! And they can't keep me there! Oh, they try—they're so tricky—but all I do is glance at the old left wrist and bingo, I remember what I'm doing! You know, everyone and their uncle will want to know about this. I mean EVERYONE, Jelly. The war office is always on at me about my inventions as it is, but they'd jolly well go mad if they knew about this. For goodness sake, DON'T tell anyone, J. I MEAN it.

I feel I need a rest soon. I've been back and forth so much, I'm beginning to feel "thin"—almost as if I don't ALL come back every time. I know they'll have my room ready in the rest home (I hate the word "asylum"—such "forever" connotations!). Just a little rest. I know I'll feel better for it. Here's a thought, old dear: If this is our legacy—the going back and forth—well then, it just stopped at some point, didn't it? I have the feeling that it all stopped when Great-Uncle Septimus died so suddenly in 1802. Remember hearing about his nosedive off the top of the church bell tower? Allenby used to frighten us with the story when WE were being too boisterous. I can hear her saying, "And then he spread his arms out and jumped straight off, just like that, shouting, "I can fly!!!" And of course he couldn't and he didn't and that was the end of him, AND—you see Jelly—he hadn't passed the secret on! From then on, no one knew! Ha! But I'm off for a bit of a rest now. I'll be better soon, old thing.

Your Tinny

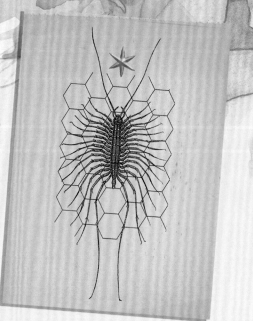

Oh, Jinny. I could keep you here and just lock you in your room again. Remember when I did that once and told Hazlett and Cook to not EVER bother you? And I didn't bother you either. I'm sorry I forgot to give you food. You DID look quite trim by the time I remembered to unlock your door. I'd remember this time — really I would. But if you go there, I'll bring you food. I promise I will. Something special.

And I DO remember Allenby telling us about Great-Uncle Septimus. What a silly man! Who ever heard of people having wings?

Your loving Jelly.

Late night

I'm going to make my own bee tattoo. The little bottle of honey, blackberry, and fairy essence ink (fairy essence???) I found is still good. That's what Quentin used, and I'm going to use it too. If I put it on my left wrist, I can do it myself. If I connect a quill pen to the generator with some string and dip it into the ink and poke myself with it, I think I can make the tattoo stay on like a real one.

Things I make seem to work here, and I don't need electricity for them either, at least not the kind I'm used to. It's still energy, but without plugs and wiring. I bet I could even get the lights to work without the fuses, but I'm not going to try, just in case! All I have to do is "know" it will work and it does. I think Quentin figured that out too—that it's all connected somehow and wires or string or whatever are only here to make us believe it works. It's magic—but it's not. It's REAL. It's fairies. I think the fairies (the little ones anyway) are the invisible stuff that holds everything together. They're in between what we see and INSIDE everything we see at the same time. It's not quantum physics, it's quantum fairies! All we have to do is believe in them! I DO believe, but I'm still going to use string.

I need the bee tattoo. I'm not sure exactly WHY you forget where you are once you're in the woods, but if the tattoo keeps you remembering, then it's important, so I'm going to do it.

Ow ow ow ow! OK, done now.

LOVE IT!

There are whole decades missing from the diary. Where did
Quentin go? There's a postcard from Belgrade and other
ones from Bucharest and Prague and Brighton too. But
they're all postmarked from somewhere in Somerset: the
Institute for the Criminally Insane and Occasional Rest
Home. Jeez. Is that what he meant by them having his room
ready? Strange...

It feels like a test. I'm supposed to be learning
something, but I don't know what it is. That's not true—I DO
know what it is. It's surviving. I think that's what
Quentin was trying to figure out—how to survive in the
"other place" and how to get back here from there without
going crazy. They went crazy—all the Cottingtons after
Great-Uncle Septimus, that is—after they went in the woods.
Or they disappeared and never came back, like the first
Flora and maybe Euphemia too. And Angelica was just crazy
anyway. Either way, it didn't work for them. But Quentin
was different. He was an inventor. Figuring things out and
making them work—that's what I'm good at too. I didn't take
robotics class for nothing!

The big fairies are so tricky. I know that now. I can feel them all the time trying to get me to come to them, to follow them into the woods, but they never let me get close enough to talk to them. Half of me wants to, but the other half REALLY doesn't!

Morning

I saw Dad again. I KNOW I did. He's hanging around outside
the gates. That's SO creepy. He KNOWS I'm here. He has to
know. Why is he just watching me? Is he making sure I'm OK?
Does he care? I don't understand. I'm NOT going out to him.

WTF is this? It was in the archives this morning. I KNOW it wasn't there before. It's me—just like in that first photo I took. JUST like it. But it CAN'T be me, can it? Oh God, maybe I DO have an evil twin!!! It's so eerie. And there they are around my head. And this was taped to it: "For you, Bright One. For things to come—future from the past—for your returning. The Fairy Painter."

Who painted this!? I can't deal with it. Does it mean "the FAIRY painter" or "the fairy PAINTER"? Painted by a fairy, or painted OF a fairy, or painted OF a fairy BY a fairy???? This is doing my head in.

I was afraid to look again because I knew what I would find. Another one. I KNEW it was there. I almost saw it before, but I just couldn't look.

OK—I looked.

It's me. It's me NOW—but it's me if I was a fairy, I think. Ha! I'm looking at the ears, and they're NOT mine. I don't have fairy ears. Is this what I'm turning into? Is it all planned out already and I'm just doing this because it's part of something preordained? Something bigger than me? It's my dad and Aunt Flora and Quentin. Poor Angelica didn't have a clue. She just pressed them. She never understood them. It's beautiful. I'M beautiful—but SO serious—and kind of cold looking. Maybe if I go with them— just walk right in with them—this is what I'd be. But I bet I wouldn't come out again. Ever.

June 21, 1938

Oh, Jinny,
   There's something I shouldn't have done.
But you've been away so often and for so long
and I've been by myself with not even Hazlett to
talk to (poor old Hazlett - he always liked you best,
you know) and Cook doesn't talk anymore and the
vicar never visits and, Oh, I don't know, Jinny.
When the nice German men came and asked
about you and the fairies and wanted to see my
pressings (I think they were very impressed!),
I told them. They weren't so nice then, and
demanded (I mean demanded - of all the cheek!)
to see your rooms and your devices and notes and
everything. I pressed a few little ones for them,
just so they could see for themselves, but they
seemed not to care at all and wanted to know how
to get into the woods. So I showed them the
beehive hut. That was bad, wasn't it? But you
weren't here, Jinny!!! You weren't here. And they
had guns, Jinny. I saw them. And now they're
gone. They went into the hut and they didn't come
back. I was watching, so I know they didn't.
I didn't tell them about that funny tattoo on your
arm. I didn't tell them that. That was good,
wasn't it, Jinny - even if the rest is really
bad?
   I hope when you return and read this you
won't be too, too angry with me. Oh dear.
                                                      J

June 25, 1938

Yes, it's all pretty bad, old girl. But you weren't to know—not really. I should have been here. I'll have to go in after them, you know. They'll forget everything once they're in deep enough, but we can't have them wandering around and stumbling upon the way back out. Too dangerous for everyone now. Much too dangerous if they take all they've found out to Germany with them. I'll be back soon, J. I've only got to lead them far enough in so they can't find their way out again—at least not out through the hut. The War Office will have to know. Don't blame yourself. I never should have told you. Silly of me, really. I think I'll be needing a rest after this. One last time in for me, and I reckon that's going to be it. I'm tired, J. I'm dog-tired.
Take care, dear sister,
Tinny

July 8, 1938
Oh, Tinny! What a beautiful arm! I wish you'd brought me one too. But why did you just come dashing out of the woods like that? Nowhere near the hut—just out and shouting all sorts of silly things. You DO need a rest, Tinny—really you DO!

XXX

 J.

Quentin must have worked for the War Office. Of course the
government would want to know about the otherworld. Well,
ALL governments would, wouldn't they—if they had proof
that it was real? That's what he meant before—but it sounds
so crazy.

TOP SECRET

WAR OFFICE
WHITEHALL
LONDON, S.W.1

Sir Henry Royds Pownall
Director of Military Intelligence

August 11, 1938

Sir Quentin Cottington
Cottington Hall
Near Mount
Somerset

My Dear *Tinny*

I write to congratulate you upon your brave and single-
handed (no pun intended here. The loss of your arm was
most unfortunate) victory over the subtle threat by enemy
spies within our most cherished heartland.

I have heard of the dreadful and hopefully
reversible state of your nerves upon returning to
Cottington Hall and I send my sincerest wishes for a
speedy recovery. We are in great need of your specialized
services during this time of profound uncertainty and
hope for your invaluable help in the near future.

As requested, I have passed your report on to Violet
Firth, that most brave and far sighted of ladies, for as
you say, she will know how best to use the information
you have provided.

Our thoughts are with you and the many years we have
served this glorious nation together in times of both
peace and war. Let not the phantoms trouble your rest.

In all sincerity,

Poodles

Later

Lost his arm??? Mental state??? The War Office never
believed him anyway. They thought he was crazy.

THAT'S what it's about—going back and forth to the
otherworld, how to go in and out. It's a Cottington thing.
It has been our secret going back to the Crusades:
traveling between the worlds. But—and here's the part that
got lost—you have to go in and especially OUT through the
beehive hut. It's like a decompression chamber: If you go
out any other way, you go crazy, or at the very least you're
changed—and not in a good way. And the bee tattoo? I bet
it's there to remind you of what you have to do to return
safely. From what Quentin said, once you go in to Faerie
(there—I'll call it what it is), you forget where you came
from and you also forget how to get out again, but with the
tattoo you can look at it and it will remind you and then
you're safe. I think that's it. I'm SURE that's it. I'm going
to try it tomorrow. I'm going to go in through the hut and
out the other door. If I come back again the same way and
I'm NOT crazy, then I'm right! That is, if the others don't
make me stay. I know they'll try to.

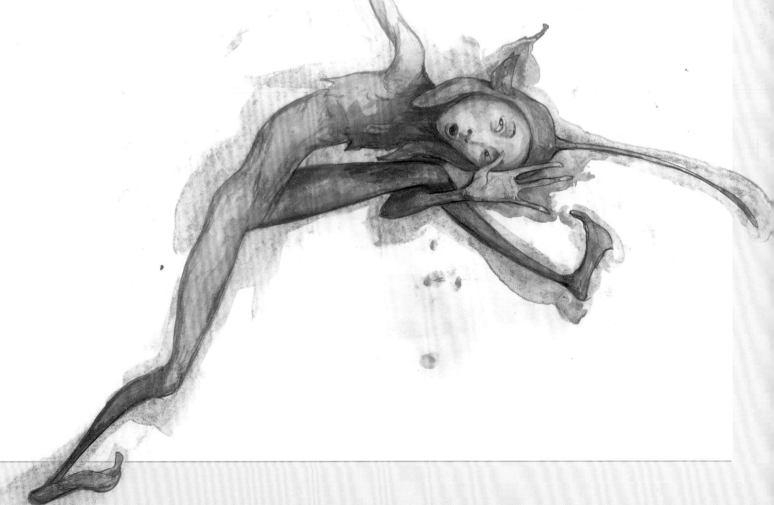

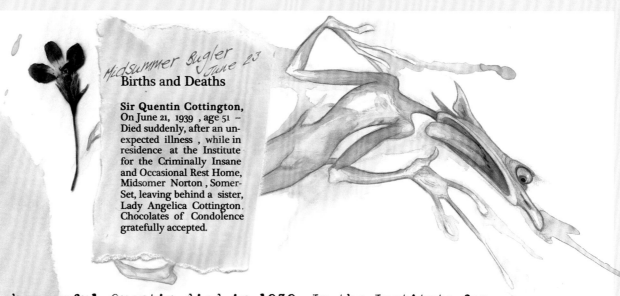

Midsummer Bugler June 23

Births and Deaths

Sir Quentin Cottington,
On June 21, 1939 , age 51 —
Died suddenly, after an un-
expected illness , while in
residence at the Institute
for the Criminally Insane
and Occasional Rest Home,
Midsomer Norton , Somer-
Set, leaving behind a sister,
Lady Angelica Cottington.
Chocolates of Condolence
gratefully accepted.

Oh, how awful—Quentin died in 1939. In the Institute for
the Criminally Insane and Occasional Rest Home.

THAT'S where he spent all those years—living there and
still doing his experiments. Oh, poor Quentin. He wasn't
insane (or criminal)! Maybe he just liked staying there—
they seemed to let him do what he wanted. He obviously
could come and go, because he came back to the Hall every
once in a while. And what about the postcards? But—I think
after going into the woods in 1938, maybe he WAS insane.
Why??? Wait, wait, wait—he lost his arm. He lost the tattoo!
That's what happened! He DIDN'T remember. He came out the
wrong way—not through the hut—and went mad finally. I
knew that was the answer! He came out with an arm made of
metal. He never acknowledged that it wasn't his real arm
(really? REALLY?). Here's a drawing of it; it says, "Arm
made by Wayland Smithy—as recompense." It's beautiful. But—
no tattoo on it.

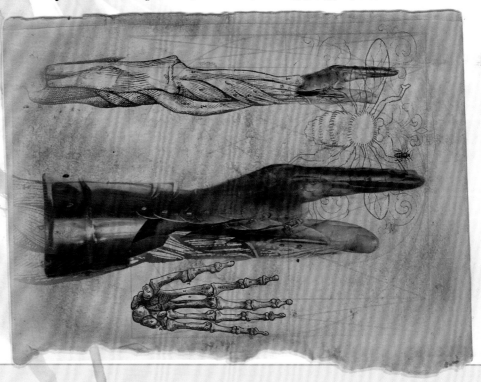

June 21, 1939

Oh, Jinny — I SO wanted to bring you a nice surprise. You always said the food was the only thing that wasn't up to snuff. I didn't know the soup would kill you — really I didn't. I know how much you love to lick the stains, so I scraped some off the tin of potted meat I opened last Christmas and put them in the soup. They looked a bit like mould, but it's the same thing, isn't it? I just wanted to make an extra special treat for you. Oh dear. I hope the stains tasted good, even if they killed you. But perhaps it wasn't the soup — they never said for certain, you know. I'm alone now, apart from the the little ones.

For the last time
Your loving Jelly.

Wow, that's so bad AND sad.

Afternoon

I hear someone pounding on the big gates. I know it's Dad.
I get the feeling he can't come into the house or onto the
grounds, but he wants ME to be here. I'll wait until he goes
away again.

I found this letter tied to the gates. He left it. He's a
coward, but at least now I know.

Dearest Maddi,

I don't know how to begin to tell you about Cottington Hall and what it means to be a Cottington, but then I don't have to, do I? You are already beginning to know what it means; I can see that.

I've watched you exploring the grounds, and I've seen you clearing away the ivy from that odd little hut. Flora and I never found it. Strange, that. We lived here until we were in our twenties but never discovered half of what I imagine you've already uncovered. I'm sure you've been in the archives. I don't remember most of the things in it, but I hope the paintings are still there. Have you found them yet? I hadn't realized until a few months ago that they were indeed of YOU — you've grown up to be the woman in the paintings. And no, I don't know who painted them — not Flora, although she was always an excellant artist—but whoever it was imagined you all those years ago—so long before you were born. Maybe it was one of them—the fairies, I mean (they have always had their own unknowable agendas)—or one of the strange people Flora and I entertained while we were in charge of the house. We had some odd friends back in those days. Wild parties. I know that's hard for you to believe of me, but it's true. We never knew what they were all up to or where they got to half the time.

When we left, Flora and I (and after the fire we HAD to leave, make no mistake about that), we promised never to talk about any of it. And we didn't. But my superiors (I can't tell you any more about them) know I'm hiding something from them. They're serious people, Maddi, and they don't play games. They want information, and they expect me to give it to them — it goes all the way back to Quentin, who seems to have worked for their associates over here in some capacity before the Second World War (the War Office has long arms and an even longer memory). So, you see? The Cottington secrets have always been desirable to people in power. They want them—whatever those secrets are—and they'll hound me until I give them up. But I can't give up what I don't know. I NEVER knew, Maddi

I had ideas, but I never really KNEW. You can see that we had to come back to England. Well, I had to come back, and I had to push YOU. I knew you felt them around you. I knew, when you showed me that first photo you took of yourself with the fairies that you would eventually have to come here—that you had a place in all of this. I also knew you wouldn't do it unless I told you NOT to, so I acted like it was the last thing I wanted you to do. You were always a stubborn little thing, and of course you ran right to Cottington Hall. And here you are. I know you so well. YOU, my dearest Maddi, are a Cottington. And that means you have fairy blood—and it IS a curse, make no mistake about it. Fiora and I lived with it for years—until we had the courage to leave. We had dealings with them, and they tried to keep us. The fairies called it love, but they CAN'T love. Oh, Maddi, their world is a WONDER. I went in once—only once, with Fiora,—and we came out changed beyond anything, perhaps even slightly mad. I could never do it again, but that one glimpse showed me such things. To have those things I'd give anything in the world, but they wouldn't let us back in. They wanted to keep us at the Hall, but they wouldn't let us back into their world. Cruel. They are cruel. We tried to burn it down, you see, but they put it out. The fairies put it out before it was destroyed completely. They want us Cottingtons here. They NEED us here, and they pull us back from wherever on this earth we try to hide. But they want us on their terms. They drive us mad, but YOU are strong. YOU are the one who will discover the secret—because there IS a secret, I know that much—and you will bring it to me, my little Maddi, because we Cottingtons can keep the secret. I don't have to give it to my superiors. It could just be between us, and if it was, then we could do SO much, Maddi—so very much, if you just tell me the secret.

So, dear girl, I'll be waiting for you here, outside the gates. I know you can do this. I've always seen it in you—that WILL to survive, to thrive.

Your loving father,
Rupert Cottington.

He's crazy!!! My dad is out of his poor, crazy, stupid mind!

He WANTED me to find out all this stuff. He KNEW I'd come if he made that crazy fuss and told me he was sending me away. Does Mom know? I bet she doesn't. I bet she is truly trying to look for me. But him? He knew. He knew all along that I'd come back here. But why can't he and weird Flora come back? Why can't they come inside? And who is it that looks like my fairy twin from all those years ago? IS it me? Is it a fairy? Who the hell am I? I always thought Dad was a strange man, but this is just insane! And who or what does he work for? Spooks? The War Office, like Quentin (speaking of insane)? I think he's just waiting for me to go into the woods and come back out still in my right mind. He doesn't know everything. He doesn't know about the tattoo. Well, I'm NOT telling him so he can go running to whoever wants to know. And if he thinks I'm going to "do his bidding" and help him rule the world (jeez, that sounds like something out of some crappy sci-fi film), he can think again. I may be Fey Maddi or Mad Maddi, but I'm ME. I'll go into Faerie on my own terms and for my own reasons. I belong there. AND I belong here. I'm going to walk between the worlds, and I'm going to stay sane.

Just found this
What IS it?

18 9
1 11
6 14
3 1 8 15
7 5
2 4 12
16 13
10

June 13.
I'm going up to the archives one more time. Maybe there's
still something important I haven't seen. There's a big pile
of stuff in the corner that I haven't even tried to look at
yet. So much stuff—but I'm going to have a dig through it
anyway, just to be sure.

I never thought to look on the back of the last painting,
but there's an envelope taped to it. OMG! It's a map with
something written on the back. It's a letter to me (or sort
of to me) from Aunt Flora.

Dearest future one,

I have seen you in my dreams. You haunt my dreams and my waking hours as well. I know you will be either my child or Rupert's, and I know that they will want you more than anything — our bargain: to let us finally leave the Hall and to have you instead. I've seen them all around you, and I've seen you in armor dressed as a dark avenging hunter. If you decide to venture into the Realm, do not enter in anger — enter with love. Rupert and I went in filled with anger, and now they won't let us enter again. They spit us out. It changed him so much, and it changed me too. Rupert and I will never speak of this again. But I understand more now. I saw the paintings (just as in my dreams) that were left here. I knew you would find them, and I knew that when you did, you would understand that they've always wanted you. I think they or their painter dreamed you into being. If you venture into Faerie, if you dare to enter, this is what you will become. You are beloved of the fairies, and they will wait for you to come to them. They told me this. They don't wish to harm you, but they DO wish to keep you. It must be your choice — to go or stay — but do not ever trust them.

Flora Cottington, 1974

Duh. No kidding. I DON'T trust them! But she's wrong. I'm NOT going to choose; I'm going to do both. I'm going to go in AND I'm going to come back out. Aunt Flora never knew the secret. She didn't know it was possible to be in both worlds, but I do.

So I'm going. I'm leaving this account here for someone else to find. Dad can't come in, so it's safe from him, but there's going to be someone who comes here someday, and when they do they'll have to understand. I won't need it where I'm going, and when I come back—and I WILL come back—I won't need it anymore either, because I'll KNOW whatever it is I need to know. I'm a Cottington and I'm NOT mad. I'm a fairy (or should it be "I'm a fairy hunter"?).

Maddi Cottington

OPEN

SHUT

Maddi C
That's me!

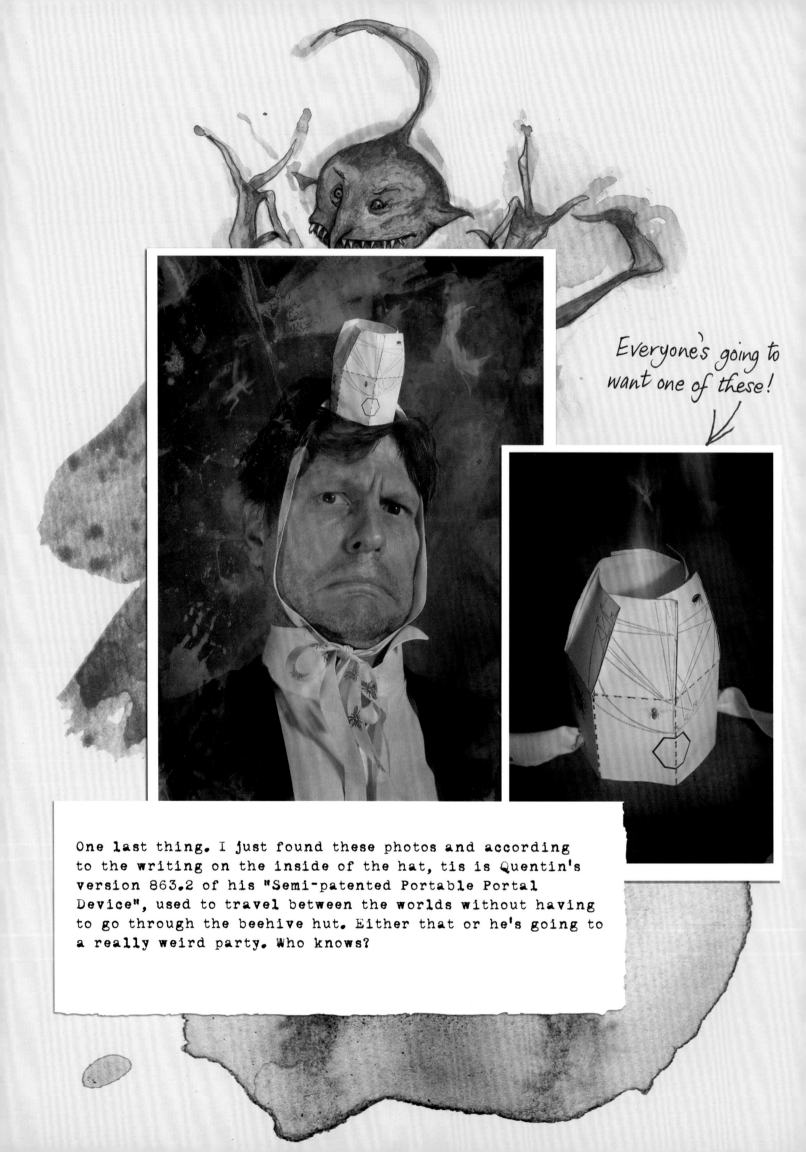

Everyone's going to want one of these!

One last thing. I just found these photos and according to the writing on the inside of the hat, tis is Quentin's version 863.2 of his "Semi-patented Portable Portal Device", used to travel between the worlds without having to go through the beehive hut. Either that or he's going to a really weird party. Who knows?

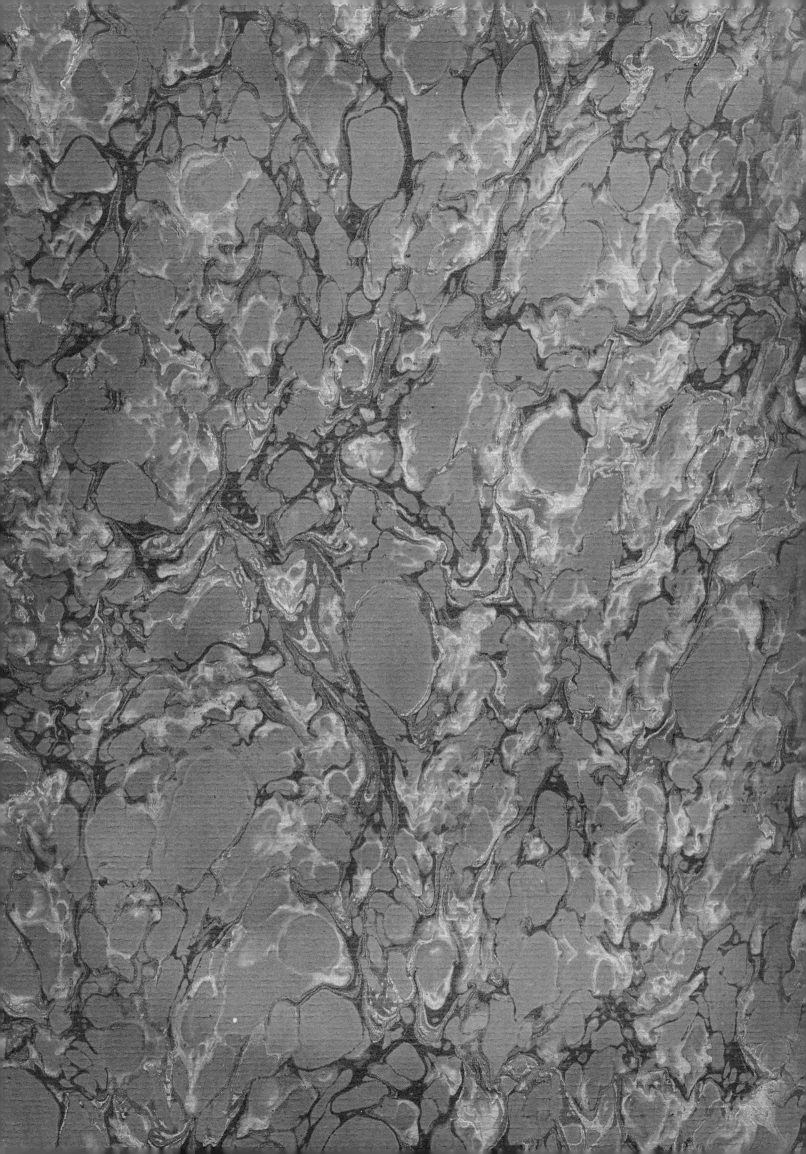